Witch Stories

ISBN 1-84135-103-2

Text copyright © 1995 Award Publications Limited
Illustrations copyright © 1995 Jane Launchbury

This edition first published 2001
3rd impression 2004

Published by Award Publications Limited,
1st Floor, 27 Longford Street, London NW1 3DZ

Printed in Singapore

WITCH AND WIZARD STORIES

Illustrated by
JANE LAUNCHBURY

AWARD PUBLICATIONS LIMITED

Contents

Curious Kevin

by Maria Gordon

Curious Kevin had set out to seek his fortune. After many miles he came to the walls of a small city. To reach the gates, he had to dodge in and out of an odd group of statues. There was a man, a donkey and a cart piled high with people, baggage and even a cat. Kevin felt a chill in their shadow. He was glad to see the gates were unguarded and he moved on, into the city.

Inside was a sorry lot of folk indeed. All moved slowly, eyes cast down, and all of them were sighing. Even stranger, Kevin noticed that across each person's nose was a sticking plaster. Curious Kevin turned to an old lady sweeping her steps.

"Excuse me, madam," he began, "but why do you all wear sticking plasters on your noses?"

"Goodness! Oh dear," cried the startled lady. "A visitor. Well, you're not excused, you know, young man. You should wear one, too, unless you want to be turned to stone."

And, as if she'd frightened herself, she gave a little shriek and ducked into a doorway, still sweeping. Curious Kevin jumped up the steps and followed her in. "Who would turn me to stone?" he asked.

"Oh dear. The wizard, of course," replied the old lady, sighing loudly as she swept.

"Tell me why," said Kevin. The old lady sighed again.

"Well, if you must know, a horrible, hairy wart has grown on the king's nose. Nothing will remove it, not even the wizard's spells. So the king covers it with a sticking plaster. Ever since, we have had to wear them, too, to stop the king feeling foolish. And if we don't, why, the wizard turns us into lumps of stone." And with that the old lady began to sweep the ceiling.

"Is your king always so silly?" asked Curious Kevin.

"Huh! You think sticking plasters are bad . . ." replied the old lady, now sweeping the windows. "Last year the king broke his leg juggling in the fountain on a Thursday afternoon. So every Thursday at three o'clock, all the men in town had to hop round the fountain until the clock chimed four."

Kevin's eyes widened. The old lady was sweeping all over, faster than ever.

"And the year before," she continued, sighing deeply, "he had all the birds turned to stone for making a mess of the palace roof and the royal statues. Everyone had to whistle for an hour at sunrise and another at sunset — or else! The king missed the birdsong, you see. Oh deary, deary me." The old lady groaned but carried on sweeping.

"Pardon me, madam," said Curious Kevin, jumping over her broom, "but why don't you move to another city with a kinder king?"

"You silly young chap. Do you think the wizard would let us?" Kevin shuddered as he remembered the stone statues outside the gates. He was glad he was only a visitor.

"I see. Well, I'd better find a sticking plaster. Where might I buy one?" he asked.

"From the wizard, of course!" said the old woman, pointing out of the window to a magnificent tower across the city. And she began sighing and sweeping so hard that Kevin had to leap out of her way and found himself back on the cobblestone street.

He frowned in thought as he made his way through the quiet, sad city to the wizard's tower. The gold railings and jewelled path showed the wizard to be a very rich man. Curious Kevin thought he knew why.

A heavy gold bell clanged as he pushed open the door.

"How can I help you?" An oily voice crept over the counter and, in the darkness, Kevin could just make out the bony figure of the wizard.

"Do you sell songbirds in cages, sir?" he asked.

"Why no, although I used to," replied the wizard.

"If I had an old boot, could you sell me one to match?" asked Kevin.

"Why, not any more, young man. You should have called last year," said the wizard.

"Then I'll just take a plaster," said Kevin.

The wizard stared nastily at Kevin before selling him a plaster for a rather high price.

"Thank you," said Kevin. Now he was sure. Every time the king had a disaster, the wizard made pots of money. The wizard sold the city folk songbirds so they didn't have to whistle and odd boots to replace ones worn out by hopping. Now it was plasters for their noses. No one could do anything about it because they'd be turned to stone.

And that, thought Kevin, could be where my fortune lies.

Grinning, he took off up the path that led to the palace. After many hours the king agreed to see him.

"Don't tell me," boomed the king, "sticking plasters give you a rash? They make your nose itch? It stings when you pull them off? Ha! If I have to wear one, then everyone does." He scowled and settled into a sulk on his throne.

"Pardon me, Your Majesty," said Kevin. "But I know how you may be rid of your wart."

"Poppycock," growled the king. "The wizard tried everything."

"Oh no he didn't," replied Kevin softly. Now the king was all ears. What Kevin had to say made him angry at first. Then he grew more and more cheerful and invited Kevin to stay overnight at the palace.

The next morning the guards were surprised to find the king chatting happily with Kevin and preparing to leave the palace.

"Right men, on your horses, please. We're off to see the royal wizard that was!" announced the king with a loud laugh. Then he cleared his throat and continued seriously, "Actually, I should warn you to be on your toes. Take care, men and, oh . . . you can take off those sticking plasters if you like." And with that, he led Kevin and the guards down to the village.

They dismounted at the wizard's tower.

"Urgent business, wizard," shouted the king. "Need something turned to stone." The wizard was down like lightning. He enjoyed his stony spell. But his face fell as he spied Kevin. Six guards surrounded the wizard in an instant and another six were sent to fetch his spell books.

"What is the meaning of all this?" hissed the wizard.

"Now, now. I have a very important job for you, wizard. I have something here that should have been turned to stone many months ago."

"And what would that be?" asked the wizard icily.

"This!" answered the king as he tore the sticking plaster from his nose (with just a tiny "ow" at the end). "This ugly wart," he continued.   "And no turning into a frog or disappearing or we'll   make sure you never see your spell books again."

The wizard saw   that he had no choice. With a nasty flash of   his gold-filled teeth, the spell was muttered.

The king's nose wiggled and his eyes crossed. The
hairy wart glowed red, then white, and snapped, falling
to the ground with a short fizz. Everyone stared at the
spiky pebble it had become. Then in dashed a chicken
who pecked it right up and swallowed it down.

"Hurray!" cheered the king and his men. Then the
king spoke firmly. "Now that," he said, "should have
happened long ago. I apologise to you all for not
thinking of this myself." He turned to the wizard. "You
may pack your bags. Then go and never return."

While all eyes were on the king, the wizard and the
wart, no one noticed as a strange glow filled the statues
outside the city gates. With a whine, a whinny and a
whimper, the donkey, the cart, a mean old money-
lender, his wife and her mother awoke once more.

"How dare you stop, you fool!" screamed the women. "Move on, move on!" And so the selfish bunch continued their escape. They gave not a glance to the city and, foolishly, did not check their baggage. Just a peep inside would have shown their hoards of gold coins still to be stone and worth not a penny. Only the cat was clever. She sneaked round the boxes, hampers and cases and jumped silently from the end of the cart. Once back outside the city, it didn't take her long to spot the new man in town and to decide that he would be hers.

Later that day, Kevin smiled as he watched the city folk dancing in the square and throwing their plasters into the fountain. On Kevin's advice, the king shared out the wizard's gold, taken so meanly from the people for birds, boots and sticking plasters. Of course, the king gave gold to Kevin, too, for breaking the wizard's hold over himself and his people. It wasn't quite a fortune, but Kevin was wise. He started a business called Palace Painters, which kept palaces and castles looking smart and kings and queens happy throughout the land. It kept Kevin very rich and his partner, a certain silky black cat from the city, very comfortable, too.

The Wildest Witch in the World

by Jane Launchbury

Grandma settled down in her favourite chair, with Jenny on her knee, and began to tell her this story:

When I was a little girl, the day I put on my witch's costume, there was big trouble.

I painted my face green, and ran into the kitchen on my broomstick, shouting, "I'm the wildest witch in the world!" My mum got such a surprise that she dropped the tea all over the kitchen floor.

"You wicked girl!" she shouted as I ran upstairs.

"I'll turn you into a toad," I said to my little brother, and made him cry.

Then I decided to make an evil spell mixture in Mum's best vase. In went all her favourite perfume, a bottle of Dad's blackest ink, most of the petals from the best rose in the garden, some hairs from the cat's tail, and a good big squeeze of stripy toothpaste.

I gave the mixture a final stir and put the vase down in the middle of the front room. Then I did a wild dance round it, on my broomstick, singing "Hubble bubble, lots of trouble!"

But my broomstick got caught in the table legs, the head fell off it, and *splat*! I fell right on top of the spell mixture. The vase broke in half and the horrible black liquid slurped all over the carpet.

Mum was furious.

"You wicked child!" she shouted. Then she sent me up to bed without any tea.

I slammed my bedroom door shut and kicked my brother's teddy across the room. If I was a real witch, I'd have a proper magic broomstick and be able to fly around the moon, I thought. Then I noticed that Mum had left the new vacuum cleaner in my room. That would do much better than a rotten old broomstick.

I clambered astride it and waved my magic wand. There was a blinding flash and a big bang. Then a strong gust of wind caught me and swept me off out of the window. I flew high over the rooftops and up towards the moon. Deeper and deeper into the night.

"Wheee," I shouted, swooping about on my vacuum cleaner. "I'm the wildest witch in the world!" Then I noticed that the sky all around me was full of witches on broomsticks. They were urging me along, faster and faster, until we all swooped down and landed in the courtyard of a great dark castle. There was a wild party going on. Hundreds of witches were doing a frenzied dance round a big, bubbling cauldron.

I joined in, screeching and wailing louder than anyone else, and prancing about so wildly that I trod on everyone's toes. The other witches thought I was the wildest witch they had ever seen and asked me to lead the dance. We danced long into the night, and I was still dancing when all the others were exhausted. They thought I must be the wildest witch in the world. So they made me their leader and asked me to cast a really wicked spell.

I thought and thought, but I couldn't think of anything that was wicked enough for the rest of the witches. They all laughed when I suggested turning little boys into toads, and they shook their heads when I suggested a spell for sending hundreds of hairy spiders into people's homes.

Then one big, fat, horrible-looking witch with yellow teeth got up and said she didn't believe that I was a real witch at all, I wasn't nearly wicked enough. She said I would have to prove myself by casting a spell.

The witches all gathered round me, gnashing their teeth and chanting. I closed my eyes tight and tried to think of something really wicked. But all I could think of was my nice, cosy home and something good for tea. All that wild prancing had made me ever so hungry.

The witches whirled round me, getting crosser and crosser. Then there was a flash and a loud bang.

"I'm s-s-sorry, I'm not really a w-w-wicked witch at all," I stammered, and burst into tears.

"I know you're not," said a familiar voice, "just a little wild sometimes."

I opened my eyes, and found myself lying on the bedroom floor, clinging on to the vacuum cleaner. Mum was leaning over me with a plate of jam sandwiches. Then she picked me up and gave me a big hug.

"I'm sorry, Mum," I sobbed.

"Never mind," she said, "I expect I'd still love you just the same, even if you *were* the wildest witch in the whole wide world."

The Forty-Niner Wizard

by Lionel Barnard

Yoni always knew he was a wizard. Ever since he could remember anything at all he had been casting spells. No one had to tell Yoni anything about wizardry; it was just like football, you could play, or you couldn't.

Yoni's spells weren't those with funny words like "hocus-pocus" and "ear of bat". It was more the way he thought about things and shaped words in his mind, although repeating words many times sometimes helped. Yoni started making spells when he was quite small. Just changing his breakfast to a strawberry milk-shake when Mother had given him porridge. Things like that. Spells made Yoni very popular at school, although wizards have to keep their spells secret.

Yoni always liked to help people and when his headmaster asked for volunteers to make visits after school to the old people's home, he was the first to put up his hand.

Now, every grown-up wizard wears a hat. It's an important rule. In olden times hats were pointed, with stars and spangles. Merlin, the greatest wizard ever, wore his pointed hat with a long cloak. But a wizard would look jolly silly walking around with those clothes now. So all the modern wizards agreed that once you were grown up you could choose your own clothes. Good wizards start to be grown up at about twelve years old.

The chief of all the wizards had given Yoni the special magic number of 49 because he had become the forty-ninth schoolboy wizard to cast forty-nine spells on forty-nine stray dogs. It was quite a feat but he managed to find lovely new homes for all the dogs in forty-nine different towns. The chief wizard said, "Congratulations, Yoni, you're a grown-up forty-niner wizard now."

As soon as he could Yoni chose his wizard clothes. A black baseball jacket and a matching cap. The cap had a long peak, to keep out the sun, and his magic number 49 on the front. On the back of the jacket he put a huge red and cream 49. He looked, well - wizard! Only other wizards would realise how important this outfit was. The chief wizard was the only one who still wore a tall black hat and carried a cane, and he said "Off you go, Yoni, you're a forty-niner wizard and no mistake."

One evening, after school, he visited his special friend Doris who lived in the old people's home. She was very old. He often thought she might know he was a wizard but neither of them mentioned it. They just chatted about the old days, when you could ride on a bus for a penny and buy chips for twopence.

That evening Doris said, "Yoni, I wish we could have fresh flowers every day, instead of these dusty paper ones. It would make us so happy."

So Yoni started thinking about a spell. The next evening he spent over two hours on his computer which had a special programme given to him by the chief wizard. After a few days the spell started to take shape and he kept a copy of it on a little magic disc, hidden in the secret pocket of his 49er jacket. He spent a few hours after school every day perfecting his spell until it was ready for its test. Every good wizard tests his spells.

On Saturday morning Yoni woke up very early and started the spell. He concentrated very hard and started calling out softly, "Florist-flowers-fresh-vases-dust-Doris-friends-always." Later on he went past the old people's home to see what had happened. Nothing, apparently, but when he walked round to the florist's he saw several old ladies sitting on the floor, covered in dust and daffodils, with vases on their heads.

The matron was there too and she was very cross. In fact she was so cross that she decided not to allow anyone out for two months, unless she found out what had happened. Doris was sitting in a corner smiling to herself. She had a secret, too.

Something had gone very wrong with the spell, so Yoni hurried home and switched on his computer. Even quite clever wizards made mistakes, he thought, but no one had been hurt. It soon became clear what had happened to make the spell go wrong. One of the wires coming out from the back of the machine was loose and a message appeared on the tiny screen saying "O wizard, you have a wire loose. Shall I try again?" There were YES and NO buttons, so as soon as Yoni repaired the loose wire he pressed the YES button. After much buzzing and a few bleeps from the computer the screen cleared. Yoni put his magic disc in the special little hole and *tap, tap,* went the keys until he was satisfied that the spell was perfect.

The next Saturday morning Yoni started the spell again. "Florist-flowers-fresh-vases . . ." The spell started working. Yoni was concentrating very hard, he must not make a mistake this time or his friends would not be allowed out.

When Yoni visited the home on Sunday afternoon Doris told him she had woken up that morning to find the dusty paper flowers had disappeared and a vase full of fresh daffodils on her table instead. Exactly the same thing had happened to forty-eight of her friends.

Matron smiled and said, "My room has been filled with bunches of red roses." Yoni smiled too, the forty-niner spell had worked. Every one was very happy, especially Yoni.

That evening Doris said, "Yoni, I know your secret –
you are a wizard. You worked that flower spell."

Yoni, who was sure his identity was still a secret,
asked how she knew.

"A long time ago," said Doris, "my husband was chief
wizard to the King of Croatia. He told me about spells
and a magic forty-niner boy, wearing the number 49. I
recognised you as a good wizard straight away, but
your secret will always be safe with me." Doris and her
friends had fresh flowers every day after that.

Yoni and Doris were friends for many years, and
she never told anyone his secret.

The Christmas Witch

by Jane Launchbury

In the darkest corner of a deep cave was a bundle of
old rags. It had been there for nearly a hundred
years, and was home to dozens of rats and spiders.
Then, one dark winter's night, the grubby mound
heaved and shuddered. A long nose emerged and
twitched, sniffing the air.

"Yummm . . . Mmmince-pies," said the bundle of rags.
The nose waggled again and then there was an
enormous sneeze that blew all the rags into the air and
sent the rats and spiders scurrying for cover.

In the gloom at the back of the cave stood a very
messy witch. She had been asleep for a hundred years
and she was very hungry indeed. Pulling on her old hat
and boots, which were full of holes and spiders, and
grabbing her broomstick, she stomped out of the cave
looking like a cross between a compost heap and a
haystack.

In the valley below, all was quiet. It was Christmas
Eve, and all the children were safely tucked up in bed.
The witch sniffed again and pointed her broomstick
towards the smell of the mince-pies. Just as she was
about to launch herself into the air there was a jingling
and a whooshing, and a fat red wizard with a pointed
hat and a long white beard flew past in a sort of sledge
pulled by reindeer. The witch stamped her foot angrily.
She did not like having a wizard on her territory so she
set off after him to see what he was up to. As she flew
she sang this song:

Scrunchy bones and scuzzy skin,
Pies with liddle childerns in,
Puppydog dumplings and roasted rats,
Mouldy mince-pies and barbecued bats.
Humdingered hamsters and spiders' legs stew,
If you don't watch out, I might eat you too!

Keeping at a safe distance, the witch watched in amazement as the wizard landed his craft on a rooftop, then, holding a bulging sack, squeezed his way into one of the chimneypots and vanished from sight. Mmm, now there's a novel way of getting into a house, thought the witch. As she landed on the roof of the house opposite, the smell of mince-pies got stronger, and without a moment's hesitation the witch dived down the chimney, just as the fat red wizard had done.

She landed with a bump in the fireplace, and a glorious sight met her eyes. The cosy room was illuminated by gently glowing coloured lights draped round a tree. There were decorations strung from everything and, most important of all, there was a huge dish of mince-pies in the middle of a beautifully laid table.

The witch headed straight for the mince-pies and stuffed them into her mouth three at a time. There was also a glass container of something that smelled rather good, so she guzzled it all to wash down the crumbs. Hiccupping loudly, she pulled down some tinsel and wrapped it round herself. Then she waltzed over to the Christmas tree and peered at her reflection in one of the shiny glass baubles. Even she had to admit that she did look a bit of a sight in her rags so she set about decorating herself.

She removed the star from the top of the tree and
stuck it to her hat, then she put some baubles on as
earrings and some more tinsel as a necklace and
bracelets. She pulled the Christmas tablecloth off the
table for a new cloak and emptied a packet of glitter
over her head. Then she stuck some pieces of holly and
paper snowflake decorations to her dress, festooned
herself with paperchains, and sat down to lace a strand
of pink tinsel through the holes in her boots. Just as she
was poking the end of the tinsel through the seventh
hole in the second boot, there was a rattling and a
rumbling and a pair of legs clad in red boots and
trousers appeared in the fireplace, followed by the rest
of the same fat man she'd seen fly past and disappear
down another chimney.

"Buzz off, wizard. I got here first," growled the witch.

Father Christmas sat in the fireplace and twiddled
his long white beard in astonishment.

The witch stood up and tried to leap forward, but she'd forgotten that she'd threaded the same piece of tinsel through both boots so she fell flat on her face in a cloud of glitter. A shiny bauble rolled across the floor and landed at the feet of Father Christmas. He frowned as he remembered stories about witches at Christmas time, spoiling the fun for everyone with spells to make people argue and burn the food. This witch hiccupped and Father Christmas chuckled to himself as he noticed the empty sherry decanter on the table.

The witch tried to get up, but got herself tangled in the paperchains. She muttered half a spell for getting rid of wizards, but it had been over a hundred years since she'd done it last and she couldn't remember the second half. The "wizard" didn't vanish.

Father Christmas surveyed the damage to the room and, keeping a wary eye on the witch who was still muttering to herself and struggling with the paperchains, he set about putting things to rights. From his bulging sack he produced a new tablecloth, a bottle of sherry to top up the decanter and mince-pies to replenish the dish. Then he put up as many Christmas decorations as the witch had removed. Finally, he produced heaps of presents from the very bottom of the sack and arranged them underneath the tree. The witch, still tangled up on the floor, grinned wickedly and twiddled her fingers at the tree. There was a red flash and one of the presents started hopping around and croaking.

Father Christmas sighed, then looked at his empty sack and had a brainwave. Quick as a flash, he popped the hopping present in, then pulled the sack over the witch's head, scooped the rest of her inside, and tied up the top with a piece of tinsel! Then he went back up the chimney with the wriggling sack and loaded it on to his sleigh.

"What am I going to do with this creature?" he asked himself as he finished his busiest night's work. The sack soon stopped struggling and started snoring, but who knew what kind of mood the witch would be in when she awoke, let alone the mischief she might make to spoil Christmas for everyone. As the first light of dawn broke and Father Christmas finished his rounds, he realised that he really only had one choice to ensure that the witch didn't start making trouble, and that was to keep an eye on her himself. He had been tempted to drop the sack on a deserted desert island, but he felt sure that it would only be a matter of minutes before the witch made herself a broomstick out of a palm tree and tried to escape.

Reluctantly, he returned to his home at the North Pole, with the sleeping witch in the sack on the back of the sleigh.

And that is how Father Christmas got himself a rather unusual helper. He soon discovered that the witch was very happy and well behaved as long as she was well fed on mince-pies and pizzas and allowed to make a certain amount of mischief. So he put her in charge of his Bad Boys and Girls department, where she is allowed to sort out special presents. Each year she has great fun as she giftwraps slugs and snails, frogs and toads, and wriggly things with loads of legs! So if you are really naughty this year, you might just wake up on Christmas morning to find that Father Christmas has left you a Christmas Witch's "special".

Village of Forbidden Magic

by Maria Gordon

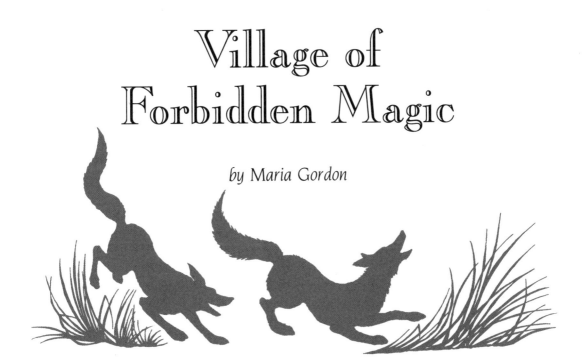

At Eleanor's touch, the swollen jaws glowed white and the deep gash shrank, then closed completely. Eleanor stroked her patient's nose. She smiled as his companions stepped forward, nudging and sniffing her in thanks. Strong Claw, their leader, was well again. The ten-year-old girl met his pale blue stare, then watched him join his pack – fifteen wolves flowing grey and white away through the long grass.

Brushing dust from her skirt, Eleanor stood up. She gazed down at her village nestling snug in the wooded valley. It held her home and the people she loved. If only she did not have to hide her magic from them.

"You're a witch, Eleanor! We saw you and that mangy wolf!" Eleanor swung round. Two younger children glared at her from the rocks where they had hidden.

"Tasmin, Luke," she greeted them softly. "Does your mother know you are so close to the wizard's lair?" The guilty spies lowered their eyes and bowed their heads. "Come, we'll return. I will not tell." She took their hands in hers and led them, smiling now, down the steep slope.

As the village path came in sight, Luke ran ahead. The wizard had hidden his trap well. Luke's cry pierced the air as the metal jaws bit deep into his leg. Eleanor and Tasmin flew to him just in time to see the steel teeth disappear in a flash at a single wave of his hand.

"I'm sorry, Eleanor. Please don't tell, please . . ."

"So you have magic, too," she said, ready to use her own to help him. But she could feel the strength of Tasmin's gaze upon the wound. The little girl said nothing. She knelt down quickly and touched her brother's ankle. The cuts sealed shut. Clouds seemed to pause and birds fell silent. A great secret had been shared.

40

The children knew magic had been forbidden in the village since long before they were born. The Magic Ones had grown selfish and greedy. They had used their power only to get more food and make their work easier. Then the evil wizard came. In return for them ignoring his wickedness, the wizard left the Magic Ones' homes and fields untouched. Their neighbours' land and houses were burnt to cinders by his dragons.

Only Eleanor's father had resisted, but his spells were not enough. He died leading a band of fighters against the wizard. The villagers agreed to pay the wizard to call off his dragons. It left them poor and many were forced to work for him, but they could stay in their beautiful land. From that day on, magic disappeared from the village. Even talk of it was banned. But now, it was clear to Eleanor, magic lived on inside the children.

Three days passed, bringing a full moon. Encouraged by its light, thirty children gathered outside the village. Eleanor stood before them. Her eyes shone with pride. She was right. From the tiniest to the tallest, all had magic. It was with them now, silencing their steps, keeping them hidden. Using their powers, together they would climb to the wizard's lair. They would tame the dragons that had helped him rule so long. Then their parents could finally stand up to the wizard. With Eleanor leading, they set off on the long climb, wrapped in warm woollen cloaks and whispered friendship.

Midnight long gone and three terrible wizard traps braved, the children reached the wizard's gloomy caverns. Using scarves to block the rank smell, they split into two groups of guards and dragon tamers. Moving in their magical silence, the tamers crept up on the sleeping dragons, chanting softly into their dreams. Unknown to them, evil bats, working for the wizard, watched their every move. Munching on moths drawn by the flickers of dragon snores, the bats flew to warn their master.

"Who dares to trespass where my dragons scare?" The angry voice shot out from the gates of the wizard's cavern like an invisible flame. Real flames snaked out, snorted by dragons crouching low beside the wizard. The children froze. Surrounding them now were twelve more newly-wakened dragons, back under their master's power. Eleanor dared to move forward, her heart beating wildly.

"We are the children of Oakwood. We ask that you free our parents from the threat of dragons and spells or . . . or . . ."

A flash lit up the wizard's sinister figure as an awful cackle pierced the air.

"Or what, you scrawny pup?"

"Or . . . we use our magic against you!" cried Eleanor. A smile twisted the wizard's face.

"So," he hissed. "Magic returns to Oakwood. Magic I can use. And what, I wonder, will your parents pay me to spare your pathetic lives?" The wizard's words fell like ice on the children's skin. "Let us ask them, shall we, children?" He raised his hand and dragon flames roared across the hillside. There in the light were the villagers, woken earlier by the warning howls of Strong Claw's wolves.

Some of the children began to cry, others cheered quietly to themselves. The dragons herded them all closer to the wizard. Still lit by dragon flare, the first parents reached the caverns.

"I am sorry, dear, puny villagers. Do my dragons make too much noise?" mocked the wizard.

"Enough, Evil One. Release our children or you shall feel the magic of Oakwood." Tamsin and Luke's father's voice was firm and low.

"Huh!" replied the wizard. "As if I fear the babblings of children and their puny powers."

"No, sir. Not theirs, but ours. Magic we once used only for ourselves. Magic we swore we'd never use again. Magic we dare now to use together!"

At this, the villagers raised their arms. A flash of blue shot into the air. It was joined by another and another until the sky above the dragons glowed like opal. A blue rain fell. One by one, the dragon flames went out. Ducking and squealing, each beast squirmed, the droplets shrivelling their scales yet leaving the children unharmed. Then every last cowardly one unfurled its wings and fled.

"What is this?" cried the wizard. Arms outstretched, he spat out spells. But each was caught by a fog of blue. His words were useless.

"You are finished here, Evil One. For years we let our magic die. Tonight we lose our shame and our children learn the truth. Leave this land or, as one, we will drive you out."

The villagers circled the wizard. He cursed, turning this way and that, shrinking, sliding into the earth until his yellow eyes glared just above it. A spray of dust and he was gone.

Parents gathered happy children.

"The truth? What did he mean?" whispered Eleanor.

"There is much to tell, child," said her mother. "But you should first know that magic never left our village."

"But why wasn't it used against the wizard?"

"Your father's death showed the Magic Ones their selfishness. They felt they did not deserve their gift and should learn to live without it."

"Until tonight."

"Tonight, we could have lost you to the wizard. But you children showed us that magic not used for good is as bad as magic used for evil. Thank you, Eleanor."

The villagers of Oakwood sang in tired celebration. Dawn lit the path home and the pale blue eyes of Strong Claw and his silent, unseen pack watched over them.

The Cat's Witch

by Jane Launchbury

In the darkness at the bottom of Molly Myrtle's garden, something stirred. Beneath the tangled undergrowth a small area of blackness, which was even blacker than the shadows, slunk swiftly through the night. Skimble the cat was on her night patrol.

Skimble, like all cats, had never been "owned" by a human. As any cat would tell you if it could speak, humans are owned by their cats. Skimble's last human had proved rather unsuitable and she was looking for somebody with better prospects.

She stretched her sleek body and sharpened her claws on the handle of a besom. Skimble gave a little purr of satisfaction. She had seen the owner of this broom and the candidate looked extremely suitable.

Skimble wanted to adopt a witch. It wouldn't matter if the woman wasn't a very good witch, or even if she wasn't a witch at all to start with, for Skimble had all the necessary magic herself.

Molly Myrtle woke early as usual and went for a bicycle ride down the country lanes. She was sad because her knees were getting old and she'd soon have to give up cycling and move to a town with good public transport.

She was surprised to find a black cat sitting on her doorstep when she got home, but she liked cats, so she let this one inside.

Molly Myrtle was not a witch, but she was rather unusual. She didn't grumble, or shout at children, she knew all the old country ways and she hated coffee mornings. Her main sadness was that she didn't have any like-minded friends. The ladies in the village all gossiped over their coffee and knitting, but that was just not Molly's scene. She had gone along once, with her own peppermint tea bag, but the other ladies had stared and whispered about her when they thought she couldn't hear them.

48

Molly soon found herself telling Skimble all this, and a lot of other things besides. The sleek black cat, who rapidly made herself at home and showed no sign of wanting to leave, seemed to be a very good listener. Of course, Molly didn't know that Skimble could understand every word she said. And it just so happened that Skimble knew a bunch of old ladies who would get on very well with Molly . . . the witches of Whitten Green.

That night, Skimble borrowed Molly's broom, purred a flying spell, and took a trip to Whitten Green. She was well-known to the cats there, and their witches, who all knew that Skimble wanted a witch of her own. They were delighted to hear about Molly Myrtle.

Over the next few days, Molly had some very unusual-looking visitors. They all arrived on broomsticks, wearing their pointed witches' hats, but tried to hide both before introducing themselves. Molly was very pleased to meet such interesting ladies, who brought their own herbal tea bags and were followed indoors by black cats, just like the one who had adopted her.

They didn't talk about witchcraft straight away, but very soon the subject of transport cropped up in conversation between Molly and the oldest lady, Griselda Flybernite. Molly was curious about how such elderly people could have walked or cycled all the way from Whitten Green, for she knew her visitors hadn't arrived in cars. And that was how they got to talking about the merits of broomstick travel and magic cats.

To start with, Molly just chuckled and gave Skimble and the old ladies some very strange looks. She had noticed that Skimble was rather unusual, but a magic cat . . ? She wasn't sure about that at all. For one thing, she kept tripping over the creature in dark corners, which didn't seem at all magical. As always, she told this to the cat, as soon as her visitors had gone. "It would be a lot easier if I could see you in the dark," said Molly.

When she woke up that night, Skimble, who was fast asleep on the end of her bed, was glowing gently. A comforting orangey colour like a nightlight.

"Skimble," whispered Molly, sitting up in bed. "Do you *really* know how to fly a broomstick?"

Skimble woke instantly, winked a green eye at the old lady, and vanished in a flash. When she reappeared, by magic, she was glowing gently like a tail-light on the end of the broomstick, which was hovering outside the bedroom window.

Molly put on her glasses and climbed out of bed to have a closer look. Then, being an old lady of adventurous spirit, she pulled on her dressing-gown and slippers, opened the window, and hopped on to the broomstick just like she hopped on to her bicycle.

It was a beautiful, starry night and Skimble took Molly on a glorious flight over the countryside. Riding the broomstick with Skimble was just as easy as riding her bicycle, but a lot easier on the knees.

Molly and Skimble soon became regular visitors to the witches over at Whitten Green. She even learned some basic spells, (though the serious magic was all done by Skimble), and that is how Molly became the cat's witch, and could live happily in her little country cottage for the rest of her long life.

Ancestral Wizardry

by Jane Launchbury

The attic stepladder creaked and wobbled as Joe climbed up to his temporary bedroom. He really didn't want to sleep on the rickety old camp-bed up there, but a matching set of elderly aunts had arrived on surprise visits and since they didn't see eye to eye about anything and refused to share the spare room, one of them had to sleep in his room.

Joe stuck his head into the attic and waggled the old light switch. Nothing happened. The attic stayed dark and dingy. Joe let his eyes adjust to the gloom. Luckily some streaks of light came through the roof where there were broken tiles. His parents were still waiting for a win in the lottery before they could afford to repair the old roof.

As he edged round the buckets and pans left there to catch drips of rain, Joe realised that there was another source of light in the attic. A pale yellow glow was coming from a wooden box which he had never noticed before.

As he made his way toward it, the glow grew brighter. Joe peered into the dusty box. The light came from something wrapped in velvet. Gingerly, he lifted the cloth. The glow from the ball he found lit the whole attic. Joe lifted it gently and set it down beside the box.

Curious, he peered into the box to see what else it held. He pulled out a tall, pointed hat covered in shiny stars and moons. It was a bit large, but he put it on anyway. Then he pulled out an enormous cloak. This was covered in the same stars and moons, which shimmered as he pulled it round himself. Underneath the cloak was the most interesting thing yet, a heavy, leather-bound book. When Joe blew the dust off, each tiny particle shimmered briefly like a little star. A shiver of excitement ran through Joe, there was something magical happening here.

Joe opened the clasp which held the book shut, lifted its cover, and gasped. There, in spidery, old-fashioned handwriting, it said:

This Book Belongs to Joseph Hamilton Stoddard.

It was his own name! How on earth had that happened? Then he remembered that he had been named after his dad's grandfather. This must have been *his* book, and his strange hat and cloak.

Lying next to the box was a black carved stick with a rounded top.

Joe ran his thumb down the carvings on the stick, and felt a tingling run up his arm. With growing excitement, he waved the stick in the air and tried saying "Abracadabra" a few times. Nothing happened. So he added the first words that came into his head:

"*Abracadabra, Kazoo Kazar, Widgemy Do Da, Blibbety Blah!*"

As he said the words, he circled the stick around his head, and the end of it hit one of the rafters holding up the roof. There was an almighty rumble of thunder, a flash of lightning, a gust of wind, and then it all went dark. Very dark indeed. Joe couldn't even see the tiniest ray of light through the broken tiles.

Joe's heart beat very fast, then he realised that the big hat had fallen over his eyes and the cloak had blown up over the hat. As he disentangled himself, he breathed a sigh of relief when he saw bright daylight. Then he froze . . . Daylight? In the attic? Joe sat down heavily on the attic floor. The entire roof had vanished! What were his parents going to say?

Spiders scuttled for cover among the dusty boxes and Joe watched them in a daze. He was too stunned even to look at the new view. What had he done?

A comforting glow still came from the ball, so he picked it up and held it. In the glow there was a swirling mistiness, and to his astonishment he saw an old man with a long white beard and a tall pointed hat. He looked familiar, and smiled kindly. He didn't speak, but he picked up a book, just like the one that Joe had found in the box, and opened it. Joe let out a gasp of amazement and his breath misted up the ball. The old man vanished completely. Joe rubbed at the ball with his sleeve, but he didn't reappear.

Maybe the old man had been trying to tell him something. Joe flipped through the pages of the book, but his excitement soon turned to disappointment.

Most of the pages were completely blank, and the writing on others was so faint that he couldn't read it. At the back there was a sort of index, but even this seemed to be mostly missing. Just as Joe was about to shut the book, a note fell out, which said:

Dear Friend,

If you can read these words, and the magic globe glows when you are nearby, then you are a true wizard. In time, you will be able to read all of this book about wizardry. When you are ready for them, the secrets and spells will become visible, To everyone else, all the words will be invisible, even these. In order to progress, you should keep your magic powers secret at all times. Good luck!

I'll need it, thought Joe, who had already tried looking up Roof Replacement in the index with no luck at all. He turned to the index again. The words that were visible were rather long ones, like thaumaturgy and caduceus and he wished he had a dictionary in the attic. He looked under R again, just in case Roof Repairing or Roof Replacement had appeared by magic. He scanned the entries quickly and found one that looked hopeful: Removals and Reinstatements.

Joe read the instructions eagerly, and discovered that it should be quite simple. All he had to do was say the words he'd used to remove the roof, backwards, while waving the stick round his head the other way. But what had he said? It had long since gone. He thought hard, and words started to form in his mind ...

Halb, Ytebbilb, Od Ad, Ymegdiw, Razak Oozak, Arbadacarba!" he said, wondering if he'd got it exactly right or not.

There was a rumble of thunder, a gust of wind, a flash of lightning, and it all went dark again. Very dark indeed. Joe felt for the hat, assuming it had fallen over his eyes again, but it hadn't. The roof had returned!

As he picked his way across the floor, past the pots and buckets, he heard a great commotion coming from downstairs. His aunts were squawking and squealing loudly. He removed the hat and cloak and climbed down from the attic. The noise was coming from the garden and his aunts were pointing up at the roof.

Joe went to see what all the fuss was about, and even he got a bit of a surprise. There was a roof on the house all right, but it wasn't the same as the roof that had been there before.

Instead of boring grey tiles there was a lovely thatched roof, and where the chimneys had been were little conical turrets!

Joe thought it looked great, but his aunts were horrified. For once they agreed about something – they were not going to stay under this spooky roof one minute longer! They packed their bags and ran off down the road.

It took Mum and Dad a while to get used to the new roof and they never did understand how it had got there, but it didn't leak, so they stopped asking awkward questions after a while. Joe kept quiet about what he'd found and done that day. In fact he has kept his wizardry skills and practise completely secret. Though whenever anyone asks him what he wants to be when he grows up, he winks and says, "I'm going to be a wizard!"